How To Handle
Your School

To Sophie
Happy reading!
Roy

Scholastic Children's Books,
Commonwealth House, 1–19 New Oxford Street,
London WC1A 1NU, UK
a division of Scholastic Ltd
London ~ New York ~ Toronto ~ Sydney ~ Auckland
Mexico City ~ New Delhi ~ Hong Kong

First published in the UK by Scholastic Ltd, 2005

ISBN 0 439 95985 3

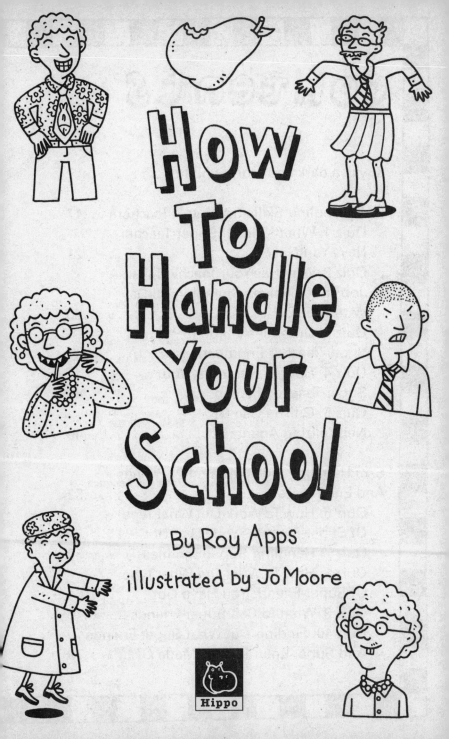

How To Handle Your School

By Roy Apps

illustrated by Jo Moore

Hippo

contents

It was a dark and stormy night 7

SAS Handling Skills Training 1: Teachers . . .17
   Quiz 1: What Kind Of Super-Teacher
   Have You Got? 21
   Quiz 2: Why Has Your Teacher Taken A
   Job That Involves Spending All Day
   With You Lot? 26
   Quiz 3: Dummies Guide To
   Super-Teacher Engineering 31
   Quiz 4: How To Neutralize Your
   Super-Teachers' Weapons 40
   Quiz 5: On The Use Of
   Neutralizing Agents 49

SAS Handling Skills Training 2: Friends
And Enemies 52
   Quiz 6: How To Work Out What Type
   Of Super-Enemies You Have Got 54
   Quiz 7: Handling Super-Enemies 59
   Quiz 8: How To Work Out What Type
   Of Super-Friends You Have Got 64
   Quiz 9: What To Call Super-Friends 70
   Quiz 10: Finding Out What Super-Friends
   And Super-Enemies Are Made Of 79

SAS Handling Skills Training
3: Headteachers 83
    Quiz 11: Hunt The Headteacher 87

SAS Handling Skills Training 4: The Man
Of Mystery 92
    Quiz 12: The Man Of Mystery 93
    Quiz 13: The Battle Of The
    Scaretaker's Cupboard 97

The How To Handle Your School Gruesome
Facts File 105

The How To Handle Your School Super
Advanced Skills Quiz Score Chart 107

The How To Handle Your School Advanced
Handler's Certificate 110

It was a dark and stormy night...
and I was snuggled up in bed dreaming
pleasant dreams about all the wonderfully
kind and useful things I'd done with my life,
like squirting shaving foam into the teachers'
coffee machine and watching them all rush
into lessons foaming at the mouth. Suddenly,
I was awoken by a noise. I leapt up with a
start and found myself staring into two large,
wild and menacing eyes.

Quickly, I wrestled my teddy on to the
floor, got out of bed and decided to go
downstairs and get myself a glass of milk.

When I got downstairs, I noticed some
strange things:

The front door
was open.

And...

There was a trail of
two sets of muddy
footprints leading down
the hall to the kitchen.

I knew this could
mean one of only two things:
Tiddles, my cat, had given up on
using the cat flap and had let herself
in the front door instead, wearing two pairs
of my wellington boots.

Or...

7

I'd got burglars.

I followed the footprints to the kitchen.
They stopped at the fridge door. Ah, now I
knew the truth! It *was* Tiddles! She had made
her way to the fridge in order to finish off the
milk that I wanted for myself!

I pulled open the fridge door.

Out leapt Tiddles, disguised as two girls
wearing Batman masks and carrying pink
and blue Super Megapower Water Pistols.

"Freeze!" yelled one of the masked
maidens.

Well, I'm not stupid.* I knew the quickest
way to obey the girl's command.
Straightaway, I leapt into the fridge's ice-cube
compartment.

---

* Dear Reader. For plenty of evidence to the contrary, please see, for
example, *How To Handle Your Teacher* or *How To Handle Your Family.* Yours
sincerely, The Publisher.

While I sat shivering in the ice-cube compartment, a thought struck me. OUCH!!!

If the two girls had been hiding in the fridge, they wouldn't be able to shoot me with their water pistols, because the water in them would be frozen!

I leapt out of the ice box.

"Ner, ner, can't shoot me! Your water-pistol water's frozen," I chortled.

"Didn't want to shoot you with our water pistols, anyway," said one of the girls with a pout.

"What did you want, then?" I asked.

"You are the World's Number One Handling Expert?" asked the girl.

I nodded. "You bet. I've written books on How to Handle Teachers, Friends, Enemies, Mums, Dads, Brothers, Sisters..."

"OK, OK," said the other girl, "we don't want your life story. We're here because we desperately need your help."

"My help," I frowned. "Mmmm, now where did I leave it? Oh yes, my help – it's upstairs in my bedroom."

The two girls ran off and I heard them clomping up the stairs. I'd got rid of them! It was so easy-peasy! Oh, how I laughed. Well, there's nothing so gleefully gigglesome as a couple of gormless girls.

Back they came.

"Did you find my help?" I asked them, still chuckling away.

"No," said one of the girls, "but you'd better help us or else."

"Or else what?"

"Or else the teddy bear gets it," said the other girl. From behind her back she produced my teddy and put the pink and blue Super Megapower Water Pistol to his head. "Once the ice in the water pistol's melted, at any rate."

"OK, OK, I'll help you," I said, "but for goodness sake, don't hurt my teddy. You see, I couldn't *bear* it."

"Aaargh," groaned one of the girls. "They warned us the jokes would be bad, but they didn't say they'd be *that* bad! Do we *have* to take him with us?"

"I'm afraid we do," said her friend.

I was bundled into the back of an unmarked white van. Well, it was unmarked when we started the journey, but by the time we finished it was very marked indeed. Mainly with impressions of my fist where I had been hammering to get out.

The journey was fast, furious and frightening, and shook every bone in my body.

"Bet this is the worst trip of your life, isn't it?" asked one of the girls.

I shook my head. "Oh no, it's nothing like as bad as the trip I took for my Cycling Proficiency Test in Year 6."

"Why, what was so bad about that?" asked the other girl.

"Ed Bashir nicked my saddle," I explained.

Eventually, the van screeched to a halt, the back doors opened and I was bundled out. I knew this could mean only one thing: we'd arrived.

Stretching out before us was a vast jungle. Exotic birds screeched in the trees and the air was hot and humid. A group of children ran to join us.

I looked up and saw a sign above my head which read:

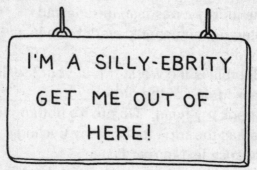

I'M A SILLY-EBRITY GET ME OUT OF HERE!

"Shouldn't that say 'I'm a *Celebrity* Get Me Out Of Here!'?" I asked.

"No," said one of the girls. She took off her mask. "Let me introduce myself," she said. "My name's Maz."

Then the other girl took off her mask.

"That's right," she added, "her name's Maz and these two lads are our mates, Chas and Naz."

Naz nodded. "And she's Daniella-Marie," he explained. "We've set up this special kids' *I'm a Celebrity Get Me Out Of Here!* We all did really well at surviving for two nights in a tank full of boa constrictors, and going for an early morning dip in our wonderful crocodile-infested lake, but there was one test that turned all four of us into jibbering wrecks."

Maz, Chas, Naz and Daniella-Marie took me over to a large hut. Above the door was a sign which filled me with gloom and foreboding.

"That sign fills me with gloom and foreboding," I said.

"It fills me with worse than foreboding," said Maz. "It fills me with *five*boding."

The sign read:

"Two things are obvious," I explained. "One, unless somebody is playing a really nasty joke, that hut is a school. And two – everybody you come across at that school in there – teachers, caretakers, dinner ladies, dodgy mates – have become immune to normal handling techniques."

"How has that happened?" asked Chas.

"It is all my fault," I admitted.

Naz grabbed hold of me. "Shall I chuck him into the croc-infested lake?" he shouted.

"Don't be so stupid," Daniella-Marie said.

Naz put me down.

"Wait till tea time when the crocs will be really hungry," Daniella-Marie added.

"Let me explain," I said. "You see, copies of my incredibly brilliant *How To Handle* books* have fallen in to the wrong hands. In other words, the hands of teachers, school caretakers and your mates."

* See footnote on page 8

"That's appalling," gasped Maz, Chas, Naz and Daniella-Marie.

"So now schools are full of a new brand of Super-Teachers and the like. There is only one way this dire situation can be sorted," I went on, "you must all go back to school with me to do some SAS training."

"Hey, cool! Does that mean we get to train with the Army?" asked Naz, excitedly.

"No, not that kind of SAS training," I explained. "This kind of SAS training is a lot tougher, scarier and more dangerous than the Army's SAS training. This SAS training is **S**uper **A**dvanced **S**chool Handling Skills Training. Well, are you up for it?"

Maz, Chas, Naz and Daniella-Marie looked uncertain.

"You'll learn how to handle school," I said.

Maz, Chas, Naz and Daniella-Marie still looked uncertain.

"You'll even learn how to handle your headteacher," I added.

Maz, Chas, Naz and Daniella-Marie didn't look convinced.

"You'll get your very own How To Handle School Advanced Handler's Certificate," I went on.

"Yeah! Cool! We're up for it!" yelled Maz, Chas, Naz and Daniella-Marie.

"Then follow me," I said.

"Where to?" asked Maz, Chas, Naz and Daniella-Marie.

"To the next page, of course," I replied.

SAS Handling Skills Training
1: Teachers

...And so the very next day, at a quarter to nine, I met Maz, Chas, Naz and Daniella-Marie round the back of the kitchens of their school, which you won't be surprised to learn was called Downwith School.

"Can't see why we can't go in the front of the school like everyone else," moaned Maz.

"Because we don't want to arouse suspicion," I said.

"Why would we do that?" asked Maz.

"For a start, you're standing there in a balaclava and camouflage fatigues carrying a pink and blue Super Megapower Water Pistol," I replied. "The first rule of SAS handling is 'don't arouse suspicion'. That's why I'm wearing the Downwith School uniform."

"Yes, but you're wearing the Downwith School *girls'* uniform," pointed out Daniella-Marie.

"Oh you're *soooooo* picky," I complained.

Half an hour later I came back wearing the *boys'* uniform.

"There, is that any better?" I asked.

"Not really," said Maz.

"Look," I retorted, crossly, "are we here to learn Super Advanced School Handling Skills or are we here to film an edition of *What Not To Wear?*"

"OK," said Maz.

"OK," said Naz.

"OK," said Daniella-Marie.

"KO," said Chas, whose spelling wasn't really up to much.

"Now the first rule of SAS handling...," I began.

"Shouldn't you tell us your name?" asked Daniella-Marie.

I stared at all four of them, straight between the eyes. "They call me," I said, "the Quizmister."

"What kind of name's that?" asked Naz, with a sneer.

"It's the sort of name for a mister who sets quizzes," I said. "Satisfied?"

Naz shrugged.

"Now let's get on your Super Advanced School Handling Skills training shall we? The first rule of which is – Remember! Not all teachers are the same."

"I'm confused," said Chas. "Half a page ago you said the first rule of SAS Handling was 'Don't arouse suspicion', now you say it's 'Remember! Not all teachers are the same.'"

Suddenly I was beginning to feel great sympathy with the teachers of Downwith School.

Eventually, I got Maz, Naz and Daniella-Marie to sit on Chas so that I could continue.

"REMEMBER! NOT ALL TEACHERS ARE THE SAME." I said once more, this time more loudly and in capital letters.

"I've never thought it about it before," said Naz, "but you're right. Like Mr Sludge has a beard, but Miss Twitty hasn't."

Mr Sludge   Miss Twitty

"No," agreed Maz, "she's got a moustache."

"There you are then," I said. "So the first SAS Handling Skill you have to learn is how to recognize what sort of Super-Teacher you have. You can do this by working out what crime(s) your Super-Teacher is guilty of when it comes to teaching you. All you need to do is to complete:

Quiz 1: What Kind Of Super-Teacher Have You Got?

The teachers on the following pages have committed the crimes described. Do any of them sound familiar? I bet they do. So, tick the boxes which apply to *your* teacher.

SUPER-TEACHER CRIME 1

TEACHER'S NAME:
Ms Erratti

CRIME:
Speeding

DESCRIPTION OF CRIME:

Ms Erratti worked her class at such a *speed* during Literacy and Numeracy hours that nobody had any energy left during morning break to do really useful stuff like kicking footballs on to the school kitchen roof or seeing whether they could twist Lenny Lickspittle's leg far enough up his back to get his big toe into his ear.

Are any of *your* teachers **GUILTY** of this dreadful crime?

YES? Tick this box ❑ And take 500 points, ie the mph speed your teacher makes you work at.

> *Now enter your points and the names of your guilty teachers in the How To Handle Your School Gruesome Facts File on p 105.*

NO? Move on to Crime 2.

SUPER-TEACHER CRIME 2

TEACHER'S NAME:
Mr Adder

CRIME:
Maths murder

DESCRIPTION OF CRIME:

The incident took place when Mr Adder made his class learn their 7 times, 9 times and 14 times tables – all before lunchtime. It was *maths murder*!

Are any of *your* teachers **GUILTY** of this dreadful crime?

YES? Tick this box ☐ And take 3 x 1 points, ie one point for every times table you have to learn.

Now enter your points and the names of your guilty teachers in the How To Handle Your School Gruesome Facts File on p 105.

NO? Move on to Crime 3.

SUPER-TEACHER CRIME 3

TEACHER'S NAME:
Mrs Biddy

CRIME: Driving with no MOT

DESCRIPTION OF CRIME:

Mrs Biddy was caught *driving* her class round the bend with no MOT: a check showed she had no brakes (no one could stop her), her spare tyre was flat and her pistons were completely worn out.

Are any of *your* teachers **GUILTY** of this dreadful crime?

YES? Tick this box ☐ And take 3 points, ie one point for every thing that the MOT found wrong with your teacher.

> *Now enter your points and the names of your guilty teachers in the How To Handle Your School Gruesome Facts File on p 105.*

NO? Move on to the next page.

Now add up all the points and enter the total score in the How To Handle Your School Gruesome Facts File on p 105.

WHAT YOUR SCORE MEANS:
Over 1,000 points: you can't count.

500–907 points: Your school is absolutely crawling with Super-Teachers. You desperately need help from an expert. So it was a lucky day indeed when you got hold of this book.

200–300 points: The Super-Teachers haven't quite got themselves into every part of your school – yet. So now's your chance to arm yourself with the skills to handle them when the dreaded day comes.

0–200 points: You're dead jammy. Keep quiet about the name of your school, or else everybody in the country will want to go there – including loads of Super-Teachers. Aaaaaargh!!!!!!

"OK, Quizmister, this Super-Teacher business is well-scary stuff," said Chas. "But what is it exactly that gives them their super powers?"

"The answer to that lies in the next two quizzes," I said. "First of all, a quiz about *why* your teacher has decided to take a job that involves spending all day with you lot."

Quiz 2: Why Has Your Teacher Taken A Job That Involves Spending All Day With You Lot?

Tick the box that you think gives the right answer.

☐   1: My teacher took a job that involves spending all day with us lot because he/she thinks my classmates (eg Lenny Lickspittle, Ali Swearah, Felicity Foulmouth, Ed Banger, Killer Sharkey, Benjamin Bogieflicker) are the most wonderful people in the world and it's a rare privilege to be working with them.

Lenny   Felicity   killer   Benjamin

☐ 2: My teacher took a job that involves spending all day with us lot because he/she thinks *I* am the most wonderful person in the world and it's a rare privilege to be working with *me*.

☐ 3: My teacher took a job that involves spending all day with us lot because he/she is ever-so slightly loopy.

☐ 4: My teacher took a job that involves spending all day with us lot because of the long holidays.

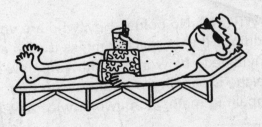

☐ 5: My teacher took a job that involves spending all day with us lot because he/she/it is an alien from the Planet Zog.

☐ 6: My teacher took a job that involves spending all day with us lot because he/she is not human.

ANSWERS:

1: WRONG. No points. I mean, come on, would you spend all day with this lot if you had any choice in the matter?

2: WRONG. No points. Hey, who are you kidding? If your teacher thinks it such a privilege to be working with you, how come he/she is sending you home with that appalling maths homework twice a week?

3: WRONG. No points. You'd have to be more than *slightly* loopy to work with your class.

4: WRONG. No points. Long holidays? What long holidays? The school holidays are far too short, as you well know.

5: WRONG. No points. If any of your teachers were aliens, they would have zapped you with their deadly hypnotizing gamma rays and whisked you off in a flying saucer to the Planet Zog long before now.

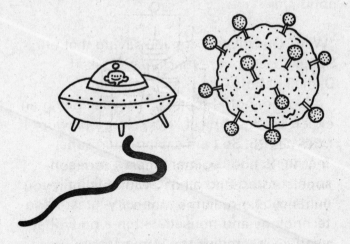

6: RIGHT!!!!!! Take 100 points. This is the only possible explanation. Any person choosing to spend all day working with you lot cannot be human.

Now add up all the points and enter the total score in the How To Handle Your School Super Advanced Skills Quiz Score Chart on p 107.

WHAT YOUR SCORE MEANS:
100 points: Brilliant! You are on the way to developing School Handling Advanced Skills.

0 points: Pathetic. In fact, your teacher very probably is an alien who has managed to turn your brain into some form of primitive pond life.

"Wow, Quizmister. Are you saying that our Super-Teachers are *machines*?" asked Daniella-Marie.

"No, I'm not," I replied, "because being an expert on the subject I never use *one* word if I can use 26. So I am saying your Super-Teacher is nothing more than a series-of-sophisticated-micro-processors-digitally-enhanced-by-means-of-the-very-latest-nano-technology-and-housed-within-a-body-that-vaguely-resembles-the-human-form."

Maz, Naz, Chas and Daniella-Marie all gasped.

"Not only that, but Super-Teachers are *military* sophisticated-micro-processors-digitally-enhanced-by-means-of-the-very-latest-nano-technology-and-housed-within-a-body-that-vaguely-resembles-the-human-form," I went on, "fitted out with precision weapons to designed to destroy your enjoyment, sleep and—"

"Mucking about?" suggested Chas. "Aaaaaaargh!!!!" he added, as Maz, Naz and Daniella-Marie all gave his shins a good kicking.

"We *never* muck about," explained Naz, with an angelic smile.

"So how do we handle these Super-Teacher machines, then?" asked Maz.

"Simple," I told her. "You learn the basics of Super-Teacher *engineering* by completing the next quiz."

Quiz 3: Dummies Guide To Super-Teacher Engineering

On the next page is a circuit diagram of a typical Super-Teacher of the most simple kind. Just match the Super-Teacher's weapons to the right letters on the circuit diagram.

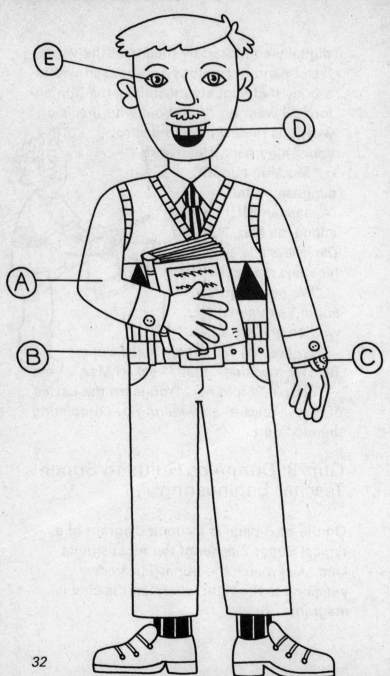

SUPER-TEACHER WEAPONS:

1: ARM-aments. Amazing weapons that enable a Super-Teacher to hold up to 30 copies of the horrific book *1,376 Really Tricky Spellings for Skools* in his/her arms at any one time and fire them one at a time to land in front of every member of your class.

2: Conveyor BELT. This terrifying piece of equipment turns your Super-Teacher into a one-man or one-woman factory, enabling them to turn out hundreds of worksheets, spelling tests, mental maths* tests, times-tables tests etc, etc day after day, week after week.

* So called, of course, because the person who thought them up must have been absolutely *mental*.

3: Risk WATCH.
Special timepiece,
developed by Time
Lord Dr Who's brother
Dr Twit T-Who, and so
called because there
is a severe risk that
this weapon could

bore you senseless. Unlike a raging bull,
which, of course, could *gore* you senseless.

| SUPER-TEACHER WITH RISK WATCH COULD BORE YOU SENSELESS | RAGING BULL COULD GORE YOU SENSELESS |

The way it works is like this: the more your
Super-Teacher *watches* their risk watch, the
more time is slowed down. That is why Literacy
Hour always seems like Literacy 24-Hours;

with this terrifying weapon, your Super-Teacher can make one hour seem like one whole day.

4: GAS bag. Enables your Super-Teacher to gas away all day* about Caesars and geezers, fractions and frictions, and twiddle and twaddle.

5: Contract LENSES. Do you ever sit in class feeling as if there is a *contract* out on your head? There is. Your teacher's amazing contract lenses enable him or her to see you making a model Stealth Bomber out of your worksheet *even though he or she is looking the other way*! Scary or what? This devilish device has been developed in partnership with gangsters from the Mafia. Except for those Super-Teachers whose contract lenses are specially

---

* And all night too, actually, because although you may not realize this, your teacher witters on about this stuff long after the bell's rung for the end of school and you and your mates have all gone home.

designed to work during Numeracy Hour. Their devices have been developed by Math-ia gangsters.*

MATH-IA GANGSTER

MAFIA GANGSTER

MUSIC TEACHER

* If your teacher does happen to be an alien (see p 28) then obviously it is his/her/its contract lenses that hypnotize you so that you can be whisked off in a flying saucer to the Planet Zog.

6: OLD SWEATER. Actually, this isn't a deadly Super-Teacher weapon, but a description of a kind of really ancient teacher, usually one that teaches PE or Games.

ANSWERS:
A = 1: ARM-AMENTS
B = 2: CONVEYOR BELT
C = 3: RISK WATCH
D = 4: GAS BAG
E = 5: CONTRACT LENSES

Take 10 points for each correct answer.

WHAT YOUR SCORE MEANS:
50 points: Well done! You have proved yourself to be a Super-Teachers' weapons expert.

30–40 points: Not bad. In fact, more like terrible.

Less than 30 points: You're not so much a
Super-Teachers' weapons expert, more like
a Super-Teachers' weapons ex-twerp.

> *Now add up all the points and enter
> the total score in the How To Handle
> Your School Super Advanced Skills
> Quiz Score Chart on p 107.*

As Maz, Chas, Naz, Daniella-Marie and I crept
along the corridors of Downwith School,
the teachers all rushed past us. There was Mr
Ha-Ha, who was a bit of a laugh, Mrs Ga-Ga,
who was beyond a joke and Miss Yah-Yah
who was a bit posh.

"When do Super-Teachers find the time
to have these deadly weapons fitted?"
asked Maz.

"There's only one time during the day
when your Super-Teachers aren't sitting in
class facing you. And that's the time Super-
Teachers *assemble* their deadly weapons.
And that's why that time is called ...
Assembly!"

"Of course!" said Naz.

"You think they are
all at the back of the
school hall, listening
to your headteacher
drone on and on,
when really they are
busy assembling their
deadly weapons! Not
only that, but three or
four times a year they close

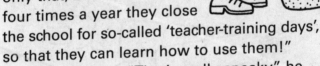

the school for so-called 'teacher-training days',
so that they can learn how to use them!"

Chas shivered. "That's really sneaky," he
said. "So how can we stop these Super-
Teachers from taking over?"

"Luckily, I have devised some simple
devices for neutralizing your Super-Teachers'
deadly weapons," I replied.

"What are these devices, exactly?"
enquired Maz.

"They're the answers to the next quiz,"
I told her.

Quiz 4: How To Neutralize Your Super-Teachers' Weapons

WARNING!!!! In order that Super-Teachers don't find out the names of the devices for neutralizing their deadly weapons, each one is written in code. The code and the answers are revealed in the upside-down footnotes at the bottom of the next page. When you have worked out the code give yourself 10 points for each correct answer and then eat the bottom of the page, so that Super-Teachers don't ever get the chance to work out the code.

Super-Teacher Weapon
ARM-AMENTS

Neutralizing Device
CINCRATA*

Super-Teacher Weapon
RISK WATCH

Neutralizing Device
MESK IF ZZZ-IRRI**

Super-Teacher Weapon
GAS BAG

Neutralizing Device
BURST POPA***

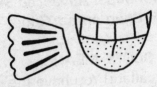

Super-Teacher Weapon
CONVEYOR BELT

Neutralizing Device
EOR REOD****

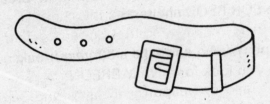

Super-Teacher Weapon
CONTRACT LENSES

Neutralizing Device
MORRIR*****

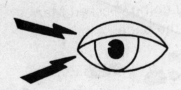 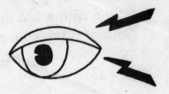

The code is: All O's have been replaced with 'I's; all 'I's with 'O's; all 'E's have been replaced with 'A's and all 'A's with 'E's.

* CONCRETE
** MASK OF ZZZ-ORRO
*** BURST PIPE
**** AIR RAID
***** MIRROR

Now add up all the points and enter the total score in the How To Handle Your School Super Advanced Skills Quiz Score Chart on p 107.

WHAT YOUR SCORE MEANS:
50 points: Axcallant! You have the makings of a Super-Teacher Handler!

20–40 points: Go and take a 30-minute break in the EOR REOD shelter.

0–20 points: Go and take a 30-*year* break while you look for a NAW BREON.

"Excuse me for asking," said Naz, "but how do you use all these things to neutralize a Super-Teacher's weapons?"
    "By following these instructions," I replied.
    "Why, where are they going?" asked Maz.
    "Along to the side of the page...

"...and back again."

SUPER-TEACHER WEAPON NEUTRALIZING DEVICES, INSTRUCTIONS FOR THE USE OF:

1: CONCRETE. Your teacher has 30 copies of *1,376 Really Tricky Spellings For Skools* on his/her desk. When they're not looking[*] pour a bucket of CONCRETE[**] over the books.

RESULT: When your Super-Teacher uses their ARM-AMENTS to lift the books, they'll blow a fuse!

2: MASK OF ZZZ-ORRO. Put on this special SAS mask[***] as soon as your teacher starts using their RISK WATCH to turn Literacy Hour into Literacy 24-Hours. It gives your face a

[*] Ie, when they're busy watching their RISK WATCHES.
[**] If you can't find a bucket of concrete, a bowl of custard from the school kitchen will do just fine.
[***] See over page.

perpetual haunting look and enables you to hide a pair of earphones behind its unique Super-Teacher-Handling Earflaps.

RESULT: You can drift off to sleep (that's why it's called the Mask of Zzz-orro) while listening to your favourite Screaming Abdabs* CDs right through Literacy 24-Hours, while your Super-Teacher thinks, by the expression on your face, that you are enjoying every moment of the lesson!

3: BURST PIPE. Your Super-Teacher's GAS BAG is a delicate piece of apparatus. Here's how to make sure it gets a burst pipe as quickly as possible.

i: PUT YOUR HAND UP.

YOU: Sir!**

* The number-one boy band, stupid.
** Obviously, if your teacher is a woman, you don't say "Sir". Unless you want to be hit on the head by a very heavy GAS BAG that is.

S-T: (WEARILY) Yes, Marmaduke, what is it?

ii: SUPER-TEACHER IS ALREADY HUFFING AND PUFFING AND POINTING AT YOUR RAISED ARM.

YOU: Oh that ... that's my arm, Sir.

iii: SUPER-TEACHER STARTS SPLUTTERING. THE PIPE TO HIS GAS BAG IS ALREADY SUFFERING FROM A BUILD-UP OF GAS AND BEGINNING TO BULGE!

S-T: I know it's your arm, you stupid boy!

YOU: Do you, Sir? Why did you ask me what it was then?

S-T: Aaaaaargh!

iv: SUPER-TEACHER'S GAS-BAG PIPE
FINALLY BURSTS.

RESULT: You don't hear another peep from
your Super-Teacher for the rest of the lesson,
which leaves you free to pursue your own
educational interests, like clicking on to the
Squidgy Bogies* website or air-kissing
Melissa Freebody in the front row.

4: AIR RAID. When you suspect your teacher
is about to use his or her CONVEYOR BELT to
get together all sorts of hideous worksheets
with spelling tests, mental maths tests and
times-tables tests on them, fling open all the
windows to let in plenty of fresh AIR.

RESULT: Every worksheet
will be blown out of the
window, leaving you free
to relax with your friends
in the comfort of your
own classroom.

*The number-two boy band.

5: MIRROR. Next time your Super-Teacher is about to use their CONTRACT LENSES to spot you day-dreaming when you should be working, make sure you have a small mirror propped up on your desk. When your Super-Teacher turns round to tell you off, they will be met, not by your startled and terrified face, but their own grisly face in the MIRROR! They will say "Stop staring at me with that ridiculous expression, or else I'll keep you in at break!"

RESULT: Your Super-Teacher has to keep himself/herself in at break!

Quiz 5: On The Use Of Neutralizing Agents

Miss Sue Perdooper's class has rigged up the classroom to enable them to neutralize her Super-Teacher weapons as quickly as possible. Can you spot the *four* handy things the class has planted before Miss Sue Perdooper does?

Take 10 points for every Super-Teacher weapon neutralizing device or tool you found (answers at the bottom of the page).

Now add up all the points and enter the total score in the How To Handle Your School Super Advanced Skills Quiz Score Chart on p 107.

WHAT YOUR SCORE MEANS:
40 points: Brilliant! You're turning into a first-class Super-Teacher Handler!

20–30 points: Not bad! If you keep at it you could soon be at the top of the class!

0–10 points: If you keep at it you, too, could soon be at the top of the class (hanging from the ceiling with the Viking helmet mobiles).

1: A concrete mixer (on bookshelf), 2: Window handles marked open, 3: A shaving mirror (strapped to a boy's head), and 4: A Mask of Zorro hanging from the ceiling.

SAS Handling Skills Training
2: Friends and Enemies

We trudged on through Downwith School, past the school office. A strict-looking lady was standing there, with her finger on a large red button on the wall. Suddenly, there was a ringing in my ears.

"That rings a bell," I said.

"It certainly does," agreed Chas. "That is Mrs Nurdler, the school secretary, ringing the bell for break time. Quick, outside, otherwise we will all be trampled to death by stampeding hordes of school persons trying to get to the playground."

"Phew!" I said, once we were outside.

"Few? There's more than a few, there's

hundreds of people out here," exclaimed Daniella-Marie.

"Yes, but none of them are teachers, are they?" I pointed out excitedly.

"No, it wouldn't be so bad if they were," said Naz, "cos we know how to handle them now, even the Super ones. The people out here in the playground are even worse. They're our friends – and enemies – and they've all got completely beyond handling."

Maz, Naz, Chas and Daniella-Marie started weeping, wailing and gnashing their teeth.

"Din't penoc!" I implored.

"What?" they chorused.

"Sorry, I forgot. I was still using the code I taught you on page 40," I explained. "What I meant to say was DON'T PANIC!!!!! There are some particularly dodgy types of Super-Friends and Super-Enemies. There are also some particularly un-dodgy types of Super-Friends and Super-Enemies. But I have here all the advice you need."

"Where? I can't see it," grumbled Chas.

"Well, it should be here somewhere," I muttered. "Oh, silly me, I've gone and left it on the next page..."

---

* Ms Broccoli, the teacher with contract lenses who should have been on playground duty had kept herself in at break time after looking in a mirror during silent reading.

Quiz 6: How To Work Out What Type Of Super-Enemies You Have Got

QUESTION 1

You're sitting down in the school hall to eat your packed lunch of prune sandwiches, leek-and-cauliflower flavoured crisps and a pear, when suddenly you are aware of one of your Super-Enemies coming into the hall, grunting, snorting and swinging their arms along the floor in typical fashion. What happens next?

↓

DOES THIS SUPER-ENEMY

A: Sneak up to your table, sit next to you, draw your attention to the fact that someone (probably them) has hung Mr Adder up, upside down, by his conveyor belt from the lighting gantry above the school stage and then, while you are looking at this interesting spectacle, nick the pear from your lunch box.

B: Sneak past your table, slip into the school kitchen, jump into the cook's washing machine, then leap out again and hang themselves next to the tea towels on the clothes airer.

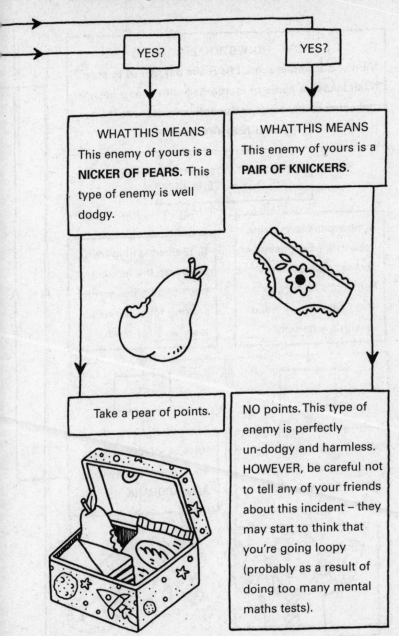

YES?

YES?

WHAT THIS MEANS
This enemy of yours is a
NICKER OF PEARS. This
type of enemy is well
dodgy.

WHAT THIS MEANS
This enemy of yours is a
PAIR OF KNICKERS.

Take a pear of points.

NO points. This type of
enemy is perfectly
un-dodgy and harmless.
HOWEVER, be careful not
to tell any of your friends
about this incident – they
may start to think that
you're going loopy
(probably as a result of
doing too many mental
maths tests).

QUESTION 2

You're out on the school field one day, about to start an innocent game of murderball with your mates, when suddenly another Super-Enemy tears past you. What happens next?

↓

DOES THIS SUPER-ENEMY

↓   ↓

A: Shove his long hairy nose into your business and say, "Oi, off the field, Lord Snooty, or else I'll bash your head in with my bare fists!"

B: Shove his long hairy nose into the football pitch and begin merrily sniffing for some nice tasty ants for lunch.

↓   ↓

YES?   YES?

↓   ↓

WHAT THIS MEANS
Your worst enemy is **AN AARDCASE** and is extremely dodgy.

WHAT THIS MEANS
Your worst enemy is **AN AARDVARK**.

Take 2 points, ie one for each of the fists that your enemy is holding up in front of your face.

NO points. This type of enemy is completely un-dodgy and harmless. Except to ants.

QUESTION 3

You're sitting about in the playground, idly sipping your can of drink as a reward to yourself after a heavy morning's work on some really mental maths, when yet another Super-Enemy approaches. What happens next?

DOES THIS SUPER-ENEMY

A: Proceed to flop down beside you with a stroppy look, grab your can of drink and swig the lot?

B: Proceed to flop down beside you with a soppy look and ... not do anything at all.

YES?

YES?

57

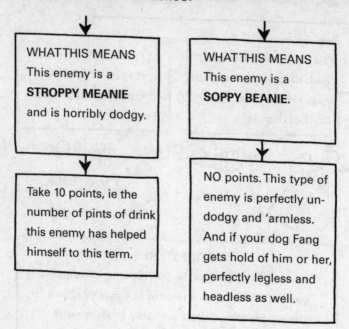

WHAT THIS MEANS
This enemy is a
STROPPY MEANIE
and is horribly dodgy.

WHAT THIS MEANS
This enemy is a
SOPPY BEANIE.

Take 10 points, ie the
number of pints of drink
this enemy has helped
himself to this term.

NO points. This type of
enemy is perfectly un-
dodgy and 'armless.
And if your dog Fang
gets hold of him or her,
perfectly legless and
headless as well.

*Add up all the points and enter the
total score in the How To Handle Your
School Gruesome Facts File on p 106.*

WHAT YOUR SCORE MEANS:
14 points: Thieves, hardcases and meanies ...
you have three well dodgy Super-Enemies.
Proceed to the next quiz without delay!
Without de-sheep, de-beanie and
de-aardvark, either.

Less than 14 points: A pair of knickers,
an aardvark and a beanie baby. You really
should be careful of the company you keep.

"So how do we handle these enemies?"
asked Daniella-Marie.

"It's as easy as doing the next quiz,"
I replied.

Quiz 7: Handling Super-Enemies

Simply put in the missing words in the
following instructions for handling the three
types of Super-Enemy described above!

A NICKER OF PEARS

1: Slice open your _____.

2: Scoop out the ____.

3: Replace with a teaspoon of _____ powder.

4: Proceed to let pear nicker ____ your pear.

MISSING WORDS:
nick pear curry stone

RESULT:
YOU SAY: Ha!

NICKER ENEMY SAYS: Aaaargh!

AN AARDCASE ENEMY

1: Take one _____ pumpkin.*

2: _____ it to look like a football.

3: When the Aardcase enemy warns you off the field, offer him the use of your_____.

4: Watch as he kicks the pumpkin and ends up with stinking ____ all over his feet and face.

MISSING WORDS:
paint mush rotting football

RESULT:
YOU SAY: Ye-e-e-h!

AARDCASE ENEMY SAYS: Eurgh!

* Or if pumpkins are out of season a large rotten water melon will do.

A STROPPY MEANIE

1: Put a can of drink in your school bag. Put school bag over your shoulder and do a 20-minute routine on a _____.*

2: At break, pretend to be enjoying your drink by saying things like "_____" and "Well delicious".

3: When Stroppy Meanie enemy demands your drink, run off with it, giving it a good _____, before handing it to him.

4: Chortle as Stroppy Meanie pulls the ring tab and _____ – he gets his face covered in fizzy drink!

MISSING WORDS:
shake delicious trampoline whoosh

RESULT:
YOU SAY: Ner, ner, ner!

STROPPY MEANIE ENEMY SAYS: Ergh, ergh, ergh!

* Or your bed, if you haven't got a trampoline.

ANSWERS:
A NICKER OF PEARS

1: Pear
2: Stone
3: Curry
4: Nick

AN AARDCASE ENEMY

1: Rotting
2: Paint
3: Football
4: Mush

A STROPPY MEANIE

1: Trampoline
2: Delicious
3: Shake
4: Whoosh

Take 10 points for every missing word you
got right.

*Now add up all the points and enter
the total score in the How To Handle
Your School Super Advanced Skills
Quiz Score Chart on p 107.*

WHAT YOUR SCORE MEANS:
120 points: Brilliant!! You're a Super Handler!

80–110 points: Not bad. You're on your way to becoming a Super Handler.

Less than 80 points: Rubbish! You're on your way to becoming a soup handler.

"That's all very helpful, Quizmister," said Maz, "but enemies are one thing."

"Glad to see your maths is up to scratch," I said.

"If the worst comes to the worst, you can always avoid an enemy. But friends aren't quite so easy to avoid, 'cos they tend to be hanging about with you most of the time."

"Exactly," I said. "You and your friends are just like the Reception Class all doing gluing, ie you stick together. But worry not. The next section of this handy handling handbook offers you helpful hints on handling the four most common types of dodgy Super-Friends, and how to tell them apart from un-dodgy Super-Friends."

Quiz 8: How To Work Out What Type Of Super-Friends You Have Got

QUESTION 1
Your Super-Friend takes you aside in the playground and says, "Hey, do you want to hear a really good joke?" What happens next?

↓

DOES YOUR SUPER-FRIEND SAY

↙ ↘

A: "What has 50 legs and can't walk? Half a centipede."

B: "If I find you snooping around Gotham City again I'll rip your fancy cape off and shove it down your throat."

YES?

YES?

WHAT THIS MEANS
Your Super-Friend is **A JOKER**, which means they are forever trying to tell you dreadful and dodgy jokes about centipedes, elephants and bananas.

WHAT THIS MEANS
Your friend is *THE* JOKER. Which means your name must be Batman. In which case, you're the dodgy one. I mean, that cape it's soooo naff, and as for the stupid tights – don't you ever watch Trinny and Susannah?

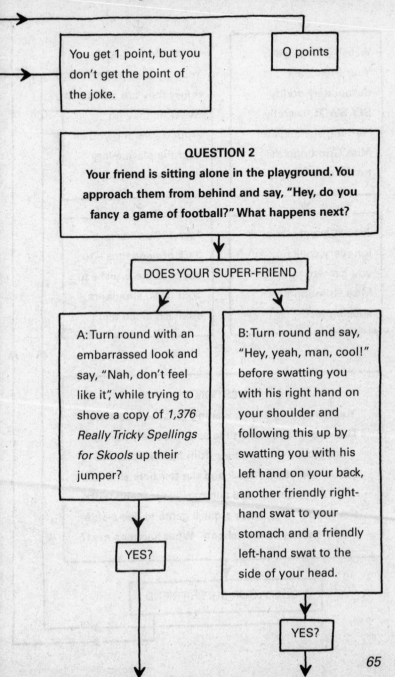

You get 1 point, but you don't get the point of the joke.

O points

QUESTION 2

Your friend is sitting alone in the playground. You approach them from behind and say, "Hey, do you fancy a game of football?" What happens next?

DOES YOUR SUPER-FRIEND

A: Turn round with an embarrassed look and say, "Nah, don't feel like it", while trying to shove a copy of *1,376 Really Tricky Spellings for Skools* up their jumper?

B: Turn round and say, "Hey, yeah, man, cool!" before swatting you with his right hand on your shoulder and following this up by swatting you with his left hand on your back, another friendly right-hand swat to your stomach and a friendly left-hand swat to the side of your head.

YES?

YES?

65

WHAT THIS MEANS
Your friend is a desperately dodgy **SLY SWOT**, secretly learning spellings for Miss Grimboggle's test after break.

WHAT THIS MEANS
Your un-dodgy friend thinks they are a **FLY SWAT**, ie they go around swatting you all over the place every time they see you.

Take 50 points, one for every spelling you get wrong in Miss Grimboggle's spelling test.

Take 100 points and a pack of bandages – to put over the bruises to your back, shoulders, stomach, head etc.

QUESTION 3
You're hanging about, waiting for school to start. This could take some time as some likely person* has nicked the batteries from Mrs Nurdler the school secretary's clock and the teachers all think it's 3.30 yesterday. You approach your friend with the words, "Hey, fancy a quick game of five-a-side widdly twinks before school?" What happens next?

DOES YOUR SUPER-FRIEND

* ie you

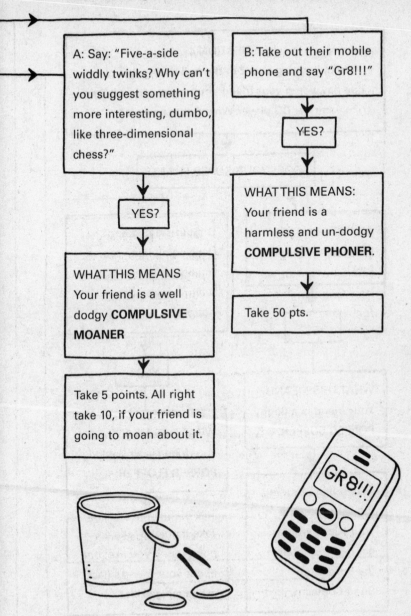

A: Say: "Five-a-side widdly twinks? Why can't you suggest something more interesting, dumbo, like three-dimensional chess?"

YES?

WHAT THIS MEANS
Your friend is a well dodgy **COMPULSIVE MOANER**

Take 5 points. All right take 10, if your friend is going to moan about it.

B: Take out their mobile phone and say "Gr8!!!"

YES?

WHAT THIS MEANS:
Your friend is a harmless and un-dodgy **COMPULSIVE PHONER**.

Take 50 pts.

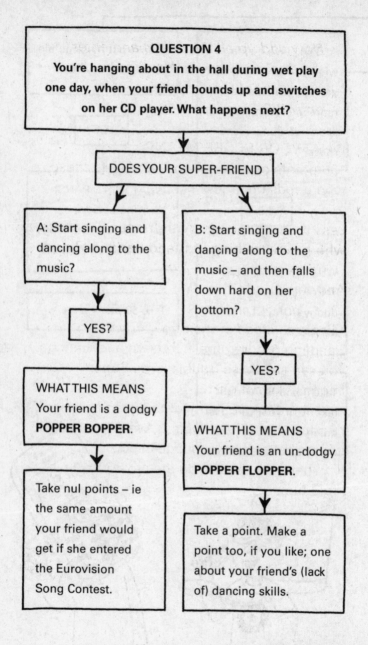

QUESTION 4
You're hanging about in the hall during wet play one day, when your friend bounds up and switches on her CD player. What happens next?

↓

DOES YOUR SUPER-FRIEND

↓   ↓

A: Start singing and dancing along to the music?

B: Start singing and dancing along to the music – and then falls down hard on her bottom?

↓

YES?

↓

WHAT THIS MEANS
Your friend is a dodgy **POPPER BOPPER**.

↓

Take nul points – ie the same amount your friend would get if she entered the Eurovision Song Contest.

YES?

↓

WHAT THIS MEANS
Your friend is an un-dodgy **POPPER FLOPPER**.

↓

Take a point. Make a point too, if you like; one about your friend's (lack of) dancing skills.

Now add up all the points and enter the total score in the How To Handle Your School Gruesome Facts File on p 106.

WHAT YOUR SCORE MEANS:
150 points or more: With friends like these, who needs enemies?

Less than 150 points: With friends like these, who needs training in friend-handling?

Answer: You do!

"The next stage of the Super Advanced Handling programme is to learn a few things you can call these troublesome Super-Friends," I went on.

"I can think of plenty of things to call them," retorted Naz. "The trouble is, we're not allowed to use that sort of language in school."

"Then you need to do the next quiz," I told him.

Quiz 9: What To Call Super-Friends

Below is a list of Super-Friend types. Against each are two nicknames. One name is appropriate, the other would spell disaster if you were to use it on a Super-Friend. Tick the name *you* think is most appropriate.

TYPE OF FRIEND	WHAT NICKNAME IS MOST APPROPRIATE?
A JOKER	❏ 1: Ha-ha-ha-rry
	❏ 2: Bunny
THE JOKER	❏ 1: Pimple Face
	❏ 2: Your Magnificence
SLY SWOT	❏ 1: Brains
	❏ 2: Brilliant/ Amazing/ Incredible

FLY SWAT

❏ 1: Bashinder

❏ 2: Duck

COMPULSIVE
MOANER

❏ 1: Primrose

❏ 2: Lisa

COMPULSIVE
PHONER

❏ 1: K8

❏ 2: Pip

POPPER BOPPER

❏ 1: Carrie

❏ 2: Lala

POPPER FLOPPER

❏ 1: Kanga

❏ 2: Ellie

ANSWERS:

A JOKER

1: HA-HA-HA-RRY. **WRONG!!!!** If you call a JOKER FRIEND Ha-ha-ha-rry they'll only think you're laughing at their jokes (some chance), which will only encourage them.

2: BUNNY. **RIGHT!** Most appropriate. After all, they're always rabbiting on and on about centipedes and elephants and bananas and stuff.

THE JOKER

1: PIMPLE FACE. **WRONG!!!!** I know it's only your idea of a joke, but the JOKER has never been one to see the funny side of things.

2: YOUR MAGNIFICENCE. **RIGHT!** Do yourself a favour and keep on the right side of this guy.

your magnificence

SLY SWOT

1: BRAINS. **WRONG!!!!** Your SLY SWOT friend won't take kindly to being compared to a nerdy puppet who wears seriously weird glasses.

2: BRILLIANT/AMAZING/ INCREDIBLE. **RIGHT!** Call your SLY SWOT friend anything along these lines and they might well let you copy their spellings in the spelling test! Cool!

FLY SWAT

1: BASHINDER. **WRONG!!!!** Say "All right Bashinder?" And your FLY SWAT friend is likely to reply "Bash in der what? Bash in der head?" And you get another swat around your head.

2: DUCK. **RIGHT!** Say "Duck!" every time you see your FLY SWAT friend and at least you'll remember what it is you've got to do.

COMPULSIVE MOANER

1: PRIMROSE. WRONG!!!! Call a COMPULSIVE MOANER friend this and they're likely to start moaning about what a soppy name it is. Particularly if the COMPULSIVE MOANER friend you've nicknamed Primrose is a boy.

2: LISA. RIGHT! What other nickname *can* you give to a MOANER except Lisa?

COMPULSIVE PHONER

1: K8. WRONG!!!! Texting type names like K8 for girl friends or S2art for boy friends or K9 for dog friends only encourages them to keep texting you instead of *talking* to you. Avoid these names at all costs, which if you're texting will probably be about £150 a minute.

2: PIP. **RIGHT!** If you say "Pip, Pip, Pip", every time you see your COMPULSIVE PHONER friend, they'll soon get the message that when it comes to texting you're continuously engaged.

POPPER BOPPER

1: CARRIE. **WRONG!!!!** If you say Carrie to a POPPER BOPPER friend, they'll immediately think you mean Carrie-okie and off they'll go again belting out soppy pop-song lyrics like "I lurv you so, my sweet/I don't mind your smelly feet" and worse.

2: LALA. **RIGHT!** If you call a POPPER BOPPER friend Lala, *they'll* think you're referring to the fact they're always singing "La-La", when in fact *you're* referring to the fact that their singing sounds like one of the Teletubbies.

POPPER FLOPPER

1: KANGA. **WRONG!!!!** If you call your POPPER FLOPPER friend Kanga, they'll say "Are you saying I dance like a kangaroo?" Which of course you are. But your friend will get sooooooo upset and start sobbing, and this sound will be even worse than their singing.

2: ELLIE. **RIGHT!** Call your POPPER FLOPPER friend Ellie and they will think it's a pretty little name. Which it is. But what they don't know, is that it's short for Elliephant. Which is what your POPPER FLOPPER friend dances like.

Take 10 points for every correct answer.

Take 5 points for every incorrect answer. Well, I feel so sorry for the trouble you are going to get into if you're twitty enough to go ahead and call your Super-Friends by these inappropriate names.

Now add up your total score and enter
it in the How To Handle Your School
Super Advanced Skills Quiz Score
Chart on p 107

WHAT YOUR SCORE MEANS:
80 points: Brilliant! What an ace nicknamer.

50–75 points: Not bad. But more of a nit-wit-
namer than a nicknamer.

Less than 50 points: You've just lost all
your friends.

The playground was beginning to empty.
"That's odd," said Chas. "Look, even the
Aarvark has given up his ant-search."

"Perhaps it's worked out that there's an
easier way to find an ant," I suggested.
"What's that?" asked Naz.
"Look for a Dec," I explained. "Because
you never see a Dec without an Ant."

Suddenly I heard a lot of groaning. At first I thought it was Maz, Naz, Chas and Daniella-Marie. Then I realized it was me. Maz, Naz, Chas and Daniella-Marie were sitting on top of me.

"Promise you won't never ever tell us any of your dreadful jokes again, ever, Quizmister!" they shouted.

I promised and they let me go.

"So, where are all our Super-Friends and Super-Enemies off to?" asked Chas.

"To have a service I expect," I replied.

"What like the Christmas Carol Service?" asked Daniella-Marie.

"They can't be!" exclaimed Naz.

"Why not?" asked Daniella-Marie.

"Because it's the middle of June," replied Naz.

"Naz is right," I explained. "Super-Friends and Super-Enemies are like cars – they need a regular service to keep going."

"Where do they go for this service?" asked Maz.

"To the school dining hall, of course," I answered.

"The school dining hall?" chorused Maz, Chas, Naz and Daniella-Marie, incredulously.

"Yes! Friends and enemies are what they eat. Just like the rest of us. Friends eat nice stuff and enemies eat nasty stuff."*

"What sort of nice and nasty stuff?" asked Naz.

"Do the following quiz and you'll soon find out," I answered.

Quiz 10: Finding Out What Super-Friends And Super-Enemies Are Made Of

Study the school dinner menu over the page and simply match the following friend and enemy fave food and drink to the correct Super-Friend or Super-Enemy.

*This is explained in more detail in How To Handle Your Enemies pp.15–16.

DOWNWITH SCHOOL
DINNER MENU

FOR MAIN COURSE

1: Karate Chops

2: Macamoanie

3: Lettuce – ie "rabbit food"

FOR PUDDING

4: Waffle

TO DRINK

5: Slime Juice

6: Loopy-zade

A: Fave food for a friend who's always *rabbiting on* on her mobile phone.

B: Fave food of a JOKER friend who's always *waffling* on and on about things like centipedes, elephants and bananas.

C: Fave food of a *tough* enemy, in other words an AARDCASE.

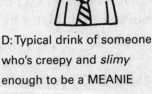

D: Typical drink of someone who's creepy and *slimy* enough to be a MEANIE enemy.

E: Just the kind of energy-giving drink for a friend who's *loopy* enough to spend all break-time reading *1,376 Really Tricky Spellings for Skools*.

F: Fave food of a real *moanie*.

ANSWERS:
1 = C, 2 = F, 3 = A, 4 = B, 5 = D, 6 = E

Take 10 points for each correct answer.

Now add up all the points and enter the total score in the How To Handle Your School Super Advanced Skills Quiz Score Chart on p 108.

WHAT YOUR SCORE MEANS:
60 points: Top of the class! Help yourself to an extra helping of chips as a reward!

Between 30 and 50 points: Not bad! Help yourself to an extra helping of cabbage as a reward.

Less than 30 points: Could do better. Help yourself to *two* extra helpings of cabbage as a reward.

SAS Handling Skills Training
3: Headteachers

"Thanks Quizmister," said Naz. "I really feel as if I'm becoming a Super Advanced school handler."

"Greeurgh," said Chas, Maz and Daniella-Marie, who were still chomping their way through their second helpings of cabbage.

Suddenly a shrill squawk pierced the air.

"Good heavens, what's that noise?" I exclaimed. "It sounds like the cry of a strangulated parrot."

"You're close," replied Maz.

"OK, I'll move back a bit," I suggested.

"I meant, you're close-about-it-being-like-the-cry-of-a-strangulated-parrot," retorted Maz, through clenched teeth. "It is, in fact, the cry of a Mrs-Nurdler-the-school-secretary. See? She's at the school doors with her beak – I mean her nose – in the air. Listen…"

"The bell's gone!" shrieked Mrs Nurdler.

Immediately, everybody in the playground

chorused, "Don't worry, Mrs Nurdler, we'll go and look for it!" And go and look for it they did. Soon, the playground was eerily quiet and empty.

"Well, there's not much more we can do out here," I said. "There's not a Super-Friend or Enemy in sight. Let's go back into the school."

As we stalked the echoing corridors, pale ghosts of ancient teachers dressed all in white floated by.

"Look!" I cried to Maz, Naz, Chas and Daniella-Marie. "Pale ghosts of ancient teachers

dressed all in white are floating by."

"They're not ghosts," said Chas. "They're dinner ladies!"

"Why have we come back into school?" whined Daniella-Marie. "We've learned how to handle Super-Teachers."

I shook my head. "There's one teacher you haven't learned how to handle yet," I explained.

We stopped outside the only door in the whole school with a decent coat of paint on it.

"What does the sign on the door say?" I asked.

```
┌─────────────────────────┐
│ ○                     ○ │
│  PLEASE KNOCK           │
│  HEAD                   │
│ ○                     ○ │
└─────────────────────────┘
```

"Argh!" said Maz.

"Ow!" said Naz.

"Ouch!" said Chas.

"Aww!" said Daniella-Marie, as they all banged their heads against the door, in accordance with the instructions.

"Do you get the impression that you are being discouraged from getting too nosey about just what's behind that door?" I asked them.

They nodded.

"It's the headteacher's office," whispered Naz in an awed voice.

"Let's go in," I suggested.

Maz, Naz, Chas and Daniella-Marie started to get their heads ready for another knocking session.

"Without knocking your heads!"
I instructed.

"What!!!!" chorused Maz, Naz, Chas and
Daniella-Marie in amazement.

"Do you want to learn Super Advanced
Headteacher Handling Skills or not?"
I enquired.

They all nodded.

"Then put your balaclavas back on and
let's GO, GO, GO!" I ordered.

Carefully, I turned the handle on the
headteacher's office door.

"Wow!" exclaimed Chas. "How did you
do *that*?"

"It's a trick I learnt on a How To Handle
Your Handle course," I explained.

I gently pushed the door open. It squeaked
a little on its hinges. I tip-toed in and
beckoned to Maz, Naz, Chas and Daniella-
Marie to follow.

What we found when we looked around
made us all gasp in astonishment.

The room was like the *Marie-Celeste*. There
were signs of recent occupation: a scattering
of papers, half a cup of cold-looking coffee,
a chewed handkerchief, teeth marks on the
edge of the desk, fingernail scratches down
the walls ... but no sign at all of a living soul.

"Where is she?" asked Chas.

"Indeed, where is she *ever*?" I agreed.
"You see, the thing about headteachers is
that they are rarely seen in school."

"Where do they go?" asked Naz.

"Do the following quiz, and you'll begin to
get some idea," I replied.

Quiz 11: Hunt The Headteacher

The picture over the page reveals places
where your missing headteacher might have
gone. See if you can match them all to the
reasons for your headteacher's absence
listed opposite the picture.

In case you need reminding what a
headteacher looks like – the chances being
that you haven't seen yours in years – here
is a picture of a couple of typical ones.

1.

2.

3.

4.

5.

6.

DR A. CULA

Which reason for your headteacher
disappearing from school, matches
which picture?

REASON:
A: "Gone to meeting with Education Chiefs
at County Hall."

B: "Gone to buy some more bats for the
school cricket team."

C: "Gone on a training course."

D: "Gone to a Head's meeting."

E: "Gone to see her favourite doctor."

F: "Gone home to do her filing."

ANSWERS:
1 = B: Your headteacher
may have gone in
search of bats, but not
the sort the cricket
team uses.

2 = A: Have you ever wondered why the
place where the Education Chiefs hang out
looks remarkably like Dracula's Castle?

3 = E: All headteachers go to Dr A Cula when they need a good jollop of medicine. It's odd, but his name looks strangely familiar, doesn't it?

4 = C: Where else do you think headteachers can get the sort of specialist training they need?

5 = D: This place is obviously stuffed full of headteachers.

6 = F: It's not her papers that your headteacher is filing, it's her teeth!

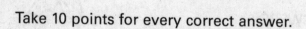

Take 10 points for every correct answer.

Now add up all the points and enter the total score in the How To Handle Your School Super Advanced Skills Quiz Score Chart on p 108.

WHAT YOUR SCORE MEANS:
60 points: Brilliant! I can see you've really got your teeth into this quiz.

20–50 points: Not bad. But, rather like your headteacher, you're still in the dark.

Less than 20 points: Terrible. If you don't watch it I can see you getting it in the neck.

Maz, Naz, Chas and Daniella-Marie gasped in horror.

"Do you mean that all headteachers are vampires?" asked Naz.

I smiled. "My lips, unlike Dracula's, are sealed," I replied.

SAS Handling Skills Training
4: The Man Of Mystery

"Phew," said Chas, after we'd left the headteacher's office far behind. "That was some scary lesson."

"Yes," I agreed, "a bit like maths. Except that's *sum* scary lesson."

I waited for the screams of protest to subside, then I went on, "Still at least the headteacher isn't the person actually *in charge* of your school."

Daniella-Marie frowned. "Well, if the headteacher isn't in charge of our school, who is?"

"You mean you don't know?" I enquired.

"If I did, I wouldn't have asked, would I?" retorted Daniella-Marie.

"We've arrived at his office now," I said.

"But we're right round the back of the school, behind the kitchens, where nobody ever goes," protested Naz.

"Exactly," I agreed. "What better place for this person to have their headquarters."

"But who is this person?" asked Maz.

"Look at the name on the door," I suggested.

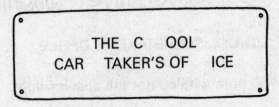

THE C   OOL
CAR   TAKER'S OF   ICE

"The Cool Car Takers of Ice? That doesn't make a lot of sense," said Chas.

"That's because, as a way of disguising where his headquarters are, this person has deliberately taken some letters off the door. See if you can fill in the missing letters and work out what the name on the door really says in the following quiz."

Quiz 12: The Man Of Mystery

Here is the sign:

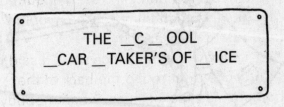

THE _C _ OOL
_CAR _ TAKER'S OF _ ICE

Here are the missing letters.

F   S   H   E   S

Can you work it out?

ANSWER:
THE **SCHOOL SCARE**TAKER'S OFFICE

Take 50 points if you got the answer right.

Give me 50 points if you got the answer wrong.

WHAT YOUR SCORE MEANS:
+50 points: Brilliant! You now know who really runs your school.

-50 points: You're probably being chased around your school hall by a maniac on the end of a giant vacuum cleaner, even as I write this.

Now enter the score in the How To Handle Your School Super Advanced Skills Quiz Score Chart on p 108.

"The School Scaretaker!" exclaimed Chas, about 15 minutes after everyone else had worked it out. "But our school doesn't have a Scaretaker, it has a *caretaker*."

I shook my head. "That's what the Scaretaker would like you to believe," I explained. "But that's just a way of lulling you into a false sense of security. You see, Scaretakers are there to *take care* of your school. Not you, nor your teachers, but the school. So they will do battle with anyone who messes it up. People like you and your teachers, who walk across their clean floors, put displays up on the walls, bring in mud from the football pitch and leave books all over their nice clean bookshelves. If you ever get to take a peep into a Scaretaker's cupboard – and I wouldn't recommend it unless you are very brave or extremely stupid – you will see that it's just like the Tardis."

"That police box used by Dr Who?" asked Naz.

I nodded. "The Scaretaker's cupboard is actually large enough inside to take weapons like brooms, brushes, mops, vacuum cleaners, floor polishers, bottles of bleach, tubs of polish, as well as a whole army of cleaners. These cleaners are people so scary and dangerous, they are only allowed in the school when everyone else has gone home."

"How can we possibly learn how to handle a Scaretaker?" asked Maz.

"By doing your school lessons properly," I replied.

"What?" chorused Maz, Naz, Chas and Daniella-Marie.

"You may think your teachers have devised all those subjects to help you in later life," I explained. "In fact, they've all been designed to help you do battle with the Scaretaker."

"How?" asked Chas.

"Do the following quiz, and all will be revealed," I said.

Quiz 13: The Battle Of The Scaretaker's Cupboard

Hidden in the Word Search below are the names of five school subjects which have been particularly designed for battles with the Scaretaker.

See how many of them you can find.

```
C  H  A  T  T  I  N  G  K  H
N  B  E  M  P  I  K  B  G  C
J  L  T  A  U  F  H  A  L  E
B  E  I  N  G  A  T  W  L  T
S  C  I  E  N  C  E  K  A  N
F  O  O  D  T  E  C  H  B  G
G  N  S  T  O  Y  H  V  T  I
S  C  U  K  T  A  L  M  O  S
M  O  A  J  R  A  P  S  O  E
F  H  S  G  A  X  K  W  F  D
```

The answers are shown opposite. Take 10 points for every subject you found.

Now enter your points in the How To Handle Your School Super Advanced Skills Quiz Score Chart on p 108.

WHAT YOUR SCORE MEANS:
50 points: Brilliant! Let battle commence (ie go straight to the next bit of the quiz).

20–40 points: Not bad. But going into battle only knowing some of your weapons will be a bit like trying to fight off a tank* with a bow and arrow.

Less than 20 points: Dodgy! Going into battle only knowing one or two of your weapons will be a bit like trying to fight off a tank with your bare hands.

* OK, so the Scaretaker doesn't actually have a tank, but he is built like one. And so is his army of cleaners.

ANSWERS:

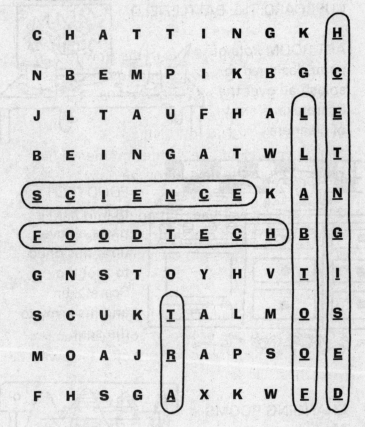

C H A T T I N G K H

N B E M P I K B G C

J L T A U F H A L E

B E I N G A T W L T

S C I E N C E K A N

F O O D T E C H B G

G N S T O Y H V T I

S C U K T A L M O S

M O A J R A P S O E

F H S G A X K W F D

"So how do these lessons help us in the Battle of the Scaretaker's Cupboard?" asked Chas.

"Study the battlefield plan over the page and you'll be able to work it out for yourselves," I replied.

THE BATTLE OF THE SCARETAKER'S CUPBOARD: THE BATTLEFIELD

ART ROOM Pots of paint designed to splash all over the Scaretaker's army of cleaners.

FOOD TECH ROOM Sticky pasta all over floor designed to root the Scaretaker and his army to the spot.

CHANGING ROOMS Mud all over floor designed squelch into the Scaretaker's battle boots.

SCIENCE LAB Specially designed electrical circuit which when tripped triggers off the fire-prevention water sprinklers, thus soaking the Scaretaker and his army with water.

DESIGN TECH ROOM Papier mache all over the tables designed to stick to the Scaretaker's and cleaners' hands and prevent them from using their weapons (ie brooms, mops etc).

"That's brilliant, Quizmister," said Maz. "Thanks so much for your help."

"All you have to do now is finish filling in your *How To Handle Your School Gruesome Facts File* and *Super Advanced Skills Quiz Score Chart*. Then as soon as you've awarded yourselves a School Handler's Certificate you can begin to put your Super Advanced School Handling Skills into practice," I said.

"We'll start first thing tomorrow," said Daniella-Marie.

"You should write a book about handling school," said Naz.

I shook my head. "My writing days are long over," I said.

"Really?" asked Maz.

"Really," I said.

I said goodbye to Maz, Naz, Chas and Daniella-Marie and went home.

A few months later I walked into our local bookshop and saw all four of them sitting behind a table. They were busily selling copies of a book. It was called...

"Hello Quizmister," said Maz, cheerily, "see, we've written a book about How To Handle School."

"Well, I never did!" I exclaimed.

"No, we know *you* didn't, that's why *we* did," explained Chas.

So I bought a copy. It only cost £3.99. And very good value it was, too.

THE HOW TO HANDLE YOUR SCHOOL GRUESOME FACTS FILE

FROM QUIZ 1 (page 21):

TEACHERS GUILTY OF SPEEDING:
NAME OF TEACHER 1:
NAME OF TEACHER 2:
NAME OF TEACHER 3:

POINTS..........

TEACHERS GUILTY OF MATHS MURDER:
NAME OF TEACHER 1:
NAME OF TEACHER 2:
NAME OF TEACHER 3:

POINTS..........

TEACHERS GUILTY OF DRIVING WITH NO MOT:
NAME OF TEACHER 1:
NAME OF TEACHER 2:
NAME OF TEACHER 3:

POINTS..........

MY TEACHERS' TOTAL SCORE................

FROM QUIZ 6 (page 54)

TYPES OF ENEMY I HAVE:
1:
2:
3:

ENEMIES' TOTAL SCORE.................

FROM QUIZ 8 (page 64):

TYPES OF FRIEND I HAVE:
1:
2:
3:
4:

FRIENDS' TOTAL SCORE.................

THE HOW TO HANDLE YOUR SCHOOL SUPER ADVANCED SKILLS QUIZ SCORE CHART

MY SCORE
FROM QUIZ 2: (page 26)

....

FROM QUIZ 3 (page 31)

....

FROM QUIZ 4 (page 40)

....

FROM QUIZ 5 (page 49)

....

FROM QUIZ 7 (page 59)

....

FROM QUIZ 9 (page 70)

....

FROM QUIZ 10 (page 79)

....

FROM QUIZ 11 (page 87)

....

FROM QUIZ 12 (page 93)

....

FROM QUIZ 13 (page 97)

....

MY TOTAL HOW TO HANDLE
SCHOOL SUPER ADVANCED SKILLS
QUIZ SCORE IS:

....

WHAT YOUR HOW TO HANDLE YOUR SCHOOL SUPER ADVANCED QUIZ SCORE TOTAL MEANS:

Over 350 points: Congratulations! You have achieved the Award of School Advanced Skills Handler (1st Class).

Between 200 and 350 points: Well done! You have achieved the Award of School Advanced Skills Handler (37th Class).

Less than 200 points: Come on! Even your TEACHER Miss Twitty* could do better than this. You have achieved the Award of School Advanced Skills Handler (Reception Class).

CONGRATULATIONS! Your unique How To Handle School Advanced Handling Skills Certificate is on the next page. Just fill in your Class.

* She's the one with the moustache, remember? See page 21.

The How To Handle Your School Advanced Handler's Certificate

This is to certify that

....

has achieved the Award of School Advanced Skills Handler

Class ....

How To Handle...

Your Mum

Your Gran

Your Dad

Your Brother/Sister

Your Teacher

Your Friends/Enemies

Your Cat/Dog

Your Mum/Dad

Grown-ups

Your Family

**Collect them all and be a
How To Handle expert!**